Time to negotiate!

Stephanie turned her attention to me again. "Lauren, you ought to be getting more privileges out of this, at least. You'll be doing a lot of adult-type stuff around your house with your mom away at her new job all day long. So will you stay up later during the week? Are you going to get more of an allowance?"

I shook my head — I hadn't thought anything through, of course.

"Now's the time to negotiate. . . . If you wait too long, your parents will start taking all of your extra work for granted," Stephanie said.

"Extra work?" I said.

"Sure, like fixing dinner, and you'll probably have to clean up the house during the week, and maybe even do some laundry. . . ."

Clean the house? I was thinking. I can't even keep my own room clean.

Look for these and other books
in the Sleepover Friends Series:

Lauren Takes Charge

Susan Saunders

AN
APPLE
PAPERBACK

SCHOLASTIC INC.
New York Toronto London Auckland Sydney

ISBN 0-590-42300-2

Copyright © 1989 by Daniel Weiss Associates, Inc. All rights reserved. Published by Scholastic Inc. APPLE PAPERBACKS is a registered trademark of Scholastic Inc. SLEEPOVER FRIENDS is a trademark of Scholastic Inc.

12 11 10 9 8 7 6 5 4 3 2   9/8 0 1 2 3 4/9

Printed in the U.S.A.   28

First Scholastic printing, July 1989

Chapter
1

"Lauren, are you serious? Your mother is actually starting a job next week?" Stephanie Green couldn't have looked more surprised if I'd said my mom was planning to run away and join the circus. "And you waited till now to tell us?"

"I didn't know myself. It was all kind of spur-of-the-moment," I replied — I'm Lauren Hunter. "Mrs. Dalton at Sawyer Insurance called her this morning and offered her a job. They used to work together a long time ago, before Roger came along." Roger's my older brother. "By this afternoon, Mom had decided to take it. She'll be the office manager there."

"Stephanie, are you going to chop those onions, or just squeeze them to death?" Kate Beekman asked.

Our sleepover was at Kate's house that Friday. She and Stephanie and Patti Jenkins and I were in the Beekmans' kitchen, trying out a new recipe from the latest issue of *Star Turns*: "Kevin DeSpain's Dynamite Date-night Chili."

"I'm chopping, I'm chopping," Stephanie muttered, putting the onions she was clutching down on the cutting board and picking up a chef's knife. "Didn't you have a fit about it?" she said, turning back to me. "I'd be absolutely hysterical!"

"*My* mother works, Stephanie," Patti pointed out gently. "Besides being a mother, I mean. And it's fine." Checking the magazine again, she said, "Lauren, we need three cups of tomatoes," and handed me a can opener.

Stephanie dropped a handful of chopped onion into the big saucepan on Kate's stove. "Yes, but your mother teaches for a few hours and then she goes home." Patti's mother is a history professor at the university. Her dad is, too. "It's not the same thing as having both of your parents gone all day long," Stephanie said. "Are you sure it's two whole onions, Kate? I wouldn't think Kevin would want to breathe onions all over his date."

Kevin DeSpain is our favorite TV star. He's the

dark-haired guy with green eyes on *Made for Each Other* every Tuesday night.

"Um-hmmm — I guess Kevin is so awesome nobody minds the onions," Kate replied, adding a tablespoon of spices to the pot. Then she held it out for me to pour in the tomatoes. "Anyway, Stephanie — about Lauren's mom — it seems to me that on a scale of one to ten of things to get hysterical about, a new kid in the family would score a lot higher than having a mother who's working."

She was talking about the fact that Stephanie's eleven years as an only child were about to come to an end — Mrs. Green's expecting a baby.

"At least Mom'll be at home where she belongs," Stephanie answered.

"I can't believe you said that!" Kate exploded.

"Said what?" Stephanie asked.

"At home where she belongs!" Kate repeated, a blonde eyebrow raised. "As if women aren't supposed to do anything except sit in the house and take care of their children! I mean, I'll probably have kids some day, but there are a lot of other things I want to do, too — like have a career!"

Kate's planning to be a movie director when she grows up.

3

"I'm going to have a career . . . ," Stephanie said with a toss of her head.

"Like what?" Kate sniffed. "Shopping doesn't exactly qualify as a career, you know," she added, pointing at the "Shop Till I Drop" button on Stephanie's sweater.

"I haven't really put my mind to it yet. I'm sure I can come up with a ton of ideas," Stephanie said breezily. "Maybe I'll be a fashion designer or something in entertainment. . . ." She shrugged her shoulders before focusing on me again. "Who's going to cook dinner at your house, Lauren? Who's going to take care of you if you're sick? Did you complain at least?"

"Well . . . no," I said. "And I don't need anyone to take care of me. Anyway, it's okay with me for Mom to work," I went on, although secretly I wasn't so sure. I was still too surprised to know *what* I thought about my mom going to work.

"You're just too easy-going," Stephanie said with a disapproving frown. "You have rights, you know. You have to learn to put your foot down, or people will run all over you."

I'd heard that a few times before, and not just from Stephanie. Kate has always been big on putting her foot down, too. In fact, she put it down just then: "Why should Lauren complain? I think it's great that Mrs. Hunter has a job!" Kate said firmly. "Now — are we making this chili, or not?"

Kate's as sure of herself as Stephanie is — according to my brother, that's why they didn't get along at first. Only he called it "bossy": "Kate and Stephanie argue because they're too much alike — both bossy."

What I'd like to know is, why hasn't some of that bossiness rubbed off on me? Why, when Roger asks me to walk Bullwinkle — even though it's raining and Bullwinkle is *his* dog, who weighs one-hundred-and-thirty pounds and can jerk me around like a yo-yo — why do I always say yes? Or when Donald Foster, only the most conceited boy in Riverhurst, whom I don't even like, but who happens to live next door to me, asks me to finish trimming the hedge so he can catch up with Wendy Rodwin on his bike, why do I say yes?

Kate and Stephanie wouldn't have any problem saying no. But I don't seem to have learned their secret.

Okay, I've only known Stephanie for a little over

a year. But Kate and I have been best friends forever — there's been *plenty* of time for her to toughen me up.

Kate and I are practically next-door neighbors — there's just Donald's house between us on Pine Street — and we started hanging out together while we were still in diapers. By the time we were in kindergarten, we'd begun to take turns sleeping over. Every Friday, either Kate would spend the night at my house, or I'd spend the night at hers.

That's when Kate's dad named us the Sleepover Twins. We'd dress up in our moms' clothes and play grown-ups, or school. Cooking in those days meant Kool Pops in the ice cube trays, with Dr. Beekman's tongue depressors for sticks.

As we got older, we graduated to Kate's super-fudge, made with a secret recipe using Marshmallow Fluf, and my own personal onion-soup-olives-bacon-bits-and-sour-cream dip, best eaten with barbecue potato chips and washed down with quarts of Dr Pepper. We watched every movie we could find on TV, played hundreds of games of Mad Libs, spied on Roger and his friends, and thought of ways to keep Kate's little sister, Melissa, from spying on *us*.

Maybe Roger's right about people who are too much alike having problems and the other way around. Kate and I couldn't be more different. For starters, Kate is short and blonde, and I'm tall and dark-haired. Kate's neat, and I'm messy. She's logical; I sometimes let my imagination run away with me. Kate has strong opinions about everything, I'm more of a waffler. But the two of us spent thousands of hours together, and in all that time we hardly ever disagreed.

Then, in fourth grade, Stephanie Green showed up. Her family had moved from the city into a house at the other end of Pine Street. I got to know Stephanie because we were both in 4A, Mr. Civello's class. She told terrific stories about her life back in the city. She knew lots about fashion and already had her own style of dressing — like mostly wearing red, black, and white. She could do all the latest dance steps. I thought she was great.

I wanted Kate to get to know her, too, so I asked Stephanie to a Friday-night sleepover at my house. *Bummer!* Kate thought Stephanie was a show-off and an airhead. Stephanie thought Kate was a stuffy know-it-all. It was pretty clear that neither of them ever wanted to see the other again.

But I wasn't willing to give up. Since all three of us live on Pine Street, we naturally started riding our bikes to Riverhurst Elementary together. Eventually Stephanie asked us to a sleepover at her house, and Kate finally agreed to go. We ate dozens of Mrs. Green's peanut-butter-chocolate-chip cookies and watched three back-to-back movie classics on Stephanie's private TV.

I don't know if it was the cookies that softened Kate up, or the triple feature, but she invited Stephanie to the next sleepover at her house. Then I asked Stephanie to mine, and then she had the two of us again, and little by little the Sleepover Twins became a trio.

Not that Kate and Stephanie suddenly saw eye to eye — far from it. I spent lots of time caught in the middle, like a referee . . . until Patti Jenkins turned up in Mrs. Mead's fifth-grade class with the rest of us. You'd never know it to talk to her — Patti's as quiet and shy as Stephanie is outgoing — but she's from the city, too. She and Stephanie even went to the same school for a couple of years.

Kate and I both liked Patti right away. She's kind and smart and thoughtful. She's also the only girl in fifth grade who's taller than I am. Stephanie wanted Patti to be part of our gang. And suddenly there were *four* Sleepover Friends!

* * *

"Anyway," I said to Stephanie, Patti, and Kate that night, "I don't think it's going to be that big a deal. Mom and Dad are going to make dinners ahead of time and freeze them. All I'll have to do is pop them in the microwave. . . ."

"After you add a few finishing touches of your own," Stephanie said, reaching for a jar of oregano on the spice rack. She sprinkled a little over the chili.

"Cut that out!" Kate said. "You're going to wreck it!"

"I am not," Stephanie said, pointing to the recipe. "Read right here: 'For extra flavor, add a pinch or two of oregano. . . .'" Stephanie's voice trailed off as she put the jar back. "I know!" she said. "I like to eat, and I like to dress up. I'll be a famous chef with a TV program, like Mavis Moore!" *Dining with Mavis* is that show on channel 31 where she cooks ten-course meals in five minutes without ever messing up her kitchen. Stephanie was going on, ". . . whip up fabulous meals on nationwide TV and then slip into a gorgeous formal — red and black — and sit down to a wonderful dinner with a bunch of stars . . . maybe even Kevin DeSpain!"

"By the time you learn to cook like Mavis

Moore, Kevin DeSpain will be a hundred and six," Kate said.

"Cooking isn't that hard," said Stephanie. "Just a pinch here and a pinch there. . . ." She sprinkled something else over the chili. ". . . and a dash of this and that. . . ." Stephanie reached for the bottle of hot sauce on the top shelf of the spice rack.

"Be careful! The spout on that's — " Kate began.

But it was too late. Stephanie had just tilted the bottle of hot sauce over the pot of chili — and the top came off! Instead of a couple of drops, about a tablespoon of the red stuff poured into Kevin De-Spain's Dynamite Date-night Chili!

". . . broken!" Kate finished with a groan.

"Oh, wow! Sorry!" Stephanie hurriedly fished the broken top out of the pot with a spoon.

"Maybe we can scoop up some of the hot sauce," Patti suggested, taking the spoon and trying to skim the blobs of reddish-orange sauce off the onions.

Kate grabbled a baster, sucked up more liquid, and squirted it into the sink. Then she stirred everything around and dipped up a spoonful for Stephanie. "I thing Mavis should try it first."

Stephanie rolled the chili around in her mouth

and raised her eyebrows enthusiastically, the way Mavis Moore does when she's sampling something she's cooked. Then she swallowed . . . and screeched at the top of her lungs, "Call the Fire Department!"

"Sssh! My dad's asleep!" Kate warned. But she started to giggle.

Patti and I were giggling, too — Stephanie's cheeks had turned a bright pink, and she was fanning her tongue with both hands as she did a fast shuffle-step with her feet. Kate poured her a huge glass of ice-cold Dr Pepper.

"I don't think cooking should be your first choice as a career," Kate said as Stephanie chugged the soda.

"Even Mavis has an accident now and then," Stephanie gasped at last. "Besides, I think I'm on to something with that hot sauce — it certainly hides the onions!"

Chapter 2

Nobody could have eaten the chili as spicy as it was, and Kate was ready to dump it. But Patti had a great idea: "If we add more meat and tomatoes, it might cool down the hot sauce. . . ."

"There's a lot of chopped meat in the freezer," Kate said. She microwaved two packages to thaw them out. Then Patti started browning the meat in the frying pan, and Kate opened another can of tomatoes.

While Kate and Patti worked on the chili, Stephanie poured herself a second glass of Dr Pepper. Then she turned her attention to me again. "Lauren, you ought to be getting more privileges out of this, at least. You'll be doing a lot of adult-type stuff around your house with your mom away all day long.

So will you get to stay up later during the week? Are you going to get more of an allowance?"

I shook my head — I hadn't thought anything through, of course.

"Now's the time to negotiate." Sometimes Stephanie sounds more like a lawyer than her father does — Mr. Green works at Blake, Binder, and Rosten, Attorneys. "If you wait too long, your parents will start taking all of your extra work for granted."

"Extra work?" I said.

"Sure, like fixing dinner, and you'll probably have to clean up the house during the week, and maybe do some laundry. . . ."

"What about Roger?" Patti asked.

"Right — he'll have to help," said Kate.

"He's got track practice every afternoon after school for the next two months, and then baseball. But Dad is going to help. He said so. . . ." I can't even keep my own room clean, much less the living room, and dining room, and kitchen, and den, and everything else!

"Let's try one more can of tomatoes," Kate said to Patti.

She stirred the extra meat and tomatoes around in the pot for a minute and then handed everybody a spoon.

Kate and Patti and I looked at the chili and then at each other. We were so slow about reaching for the pot that Stephanie sighed loudly. "I'll go first." She grabbed her Dr Pepper glass with one hand, then scooped up a spoonful of chili, blew on it, and stuck it quickly into her mouth with the other hand.

Stephanie sort of held her breath . . . and broke into a big smile. "It's excellent, as a matter of fact!" she announced. "I've turned a basically humdrum recipe into something scrumptious — I think I'm a natural chef!"

Kate rolled her eyes at Patti and me. Then she held her nose, as if she were about to take some really nasty medicine, and swallowed her chili in one gulp.

But the chili *was* good. "I'll have a bowl right now," I said after I'd tasted mine.

Kate shook her head. "Can't — it has to cook for at least forty-five minutes, to mix all the flavors together," she said.

"I'll faint from hunger by then," I groaned. "My dinner was almost three hours ago!"

"I haven't forgotten the bottomless pit. There's plenty of other stuff to tide you over," Kate said soothingly. "Two platters of super-fudge, some of

Patti's Alaska Dip, an economy-size bag of barbecue potato chips. . . ."

"That should hold me for forty-five minutes," I had to admit. I took one of the trays off the top of Kate's refrigerator and started piling it with munchies.

"I've figured out how Lauren can eat so much and stay so thin," Stephanie said. Stephanie's always talking about going on diets, although she doesn't really need to. It's just that she's short, with a round-ish face.

"How?" Kate asked her, filling another tray with plates and glasses and napkins.

"Her stomach lives somewhere else," Stephanie said solemnly. "Like outer space. All of the food Lauren eats is automatically beamed up to an asteroid or something, where there's this enormous pink stomach the size of a house, just sitting there, gurgling."

"Gross!" Kate said, but she burst out laughing. Patti was giggling, too.

"Very funny," I said, grabbing the bag of barbecue potato chips and adding it to the pile on the tray.

"Hang on, stomach — here come some chips!" Stephanie softly called up to the ceiling.

We carried the food upstairs, careful to jump over the squeaky third step from the top. Melissa had already gone to bed, and we sure didn't want to wake *her* up.

As soon as we'd gotten to Kate's bedroom and closed the door behind us, Stephanie grabbed a handful of chips and said, "Okay, Lauren — we're going to do some role-playing."

"Role-playing?" We usually play Truth or Dare at our sleepovers, so I wasn't sure what Stephanie had in mind. Did this have anything to do with Stephanie choosing a career?

Stephanie went on, "I'll be your mom, and you be you."

"You're kidding!" said Kate. She and Patti had sat down on the floor and were unloading the trays, but they both stopped to stare at Stephanie.

"I saw it on a TV talk show," Stephanie said. "You act out all the things that might happen in a certain situation ahead of time, and that way you have the advantage. I'm your mom. . . ." Stephanie lowered her voice, "Lauren, as you know, I'll be going back to work on Monday. During the week I'll expect you to set the table, cook dinner, vacuum the house on Tuesdays and Thursdays . . . and do several other chores. . . ." Stephanie paused, looking at me.

When I didn't say anything, she waved her hands at me. "Go ahead. Start with, 'Listen, Mom,' " she suggested.

"Listen, Mom," I repeated, but I couldn't think of anything else to say, mainly because "Listen, Mom," didn't sound like me.

"You don't talk like that to your mother," Kate pointed out. "You don't even talk that way to Bullwinkle."

Stephanie sighed impatiently. "Then say what you *would* say, Lauren."

I thought for a second. "Uh . . . Mom . . . there's something . . . ," I began again, but then I started to giggle.

My mom has pale skin and straight, light-brown hair that she wears pulled back. Stephanie has short black curls, and olive skin. My mom has kind of a long, bony face. Stephanie is always sucking her cheeks in to try to *find* bones in hers. Besides, my mom is almost five-nine, and I tower over Stephanie. "I . . . I guess I don't have a g-good enough imagination," I stammered through my giggles as Stephanie scowled at me.

"I'll do your part, then," she told me. "Listen, Mom — since I didn't have any say in whether or not you should go back to work — and since it'll mean a lot more responsibilities for me — I think it's only fair that you raise my allowance by two dollars a week at the very least. I also think I should be able to stay up an extra hour at night, because all of the housework I'll be doing will take away from my free time. . . ."

"Right about now, my mother would say, 'That's enough, young lady. I think your allowance is more than fair for a fifth-grader' " — I get three dollars and fifty cents a week. "Then she'd say, 'One of the reasons I'm going back to work is to put money in the bank for college for you and Roger.' "

"Good, good!" Stephanie approved of my performance as my mom. "Then you — Lauren — will say, 'But the extra hour a night won't take anything away from the college fund, and — ' "

"I don't know," I said doubtfully. I mean, I love my parents, but they're a lot stricter with me than Stephanie's are with her.

"Give it a rest, Stephanie," Kate said. "Lauren has to decide whether or not she wants to say anything at all to her parents. Have some Alaska Dip," she said, holding the bowl out to Stephanie.

"Just trying to help," Stephanie said, sitting down on the floor next to Kate and scooping up a big chip-ful of the tuna dip.

"And I appreciate it," I told her. An extra hour at night did sound good — maybe I would talk to Mom.

"Want to see who's on the *Video Trax Live* concert?" Patti asked.

Video Trax plays rock videos most of the time, but on Friday and Saturday nights they carry live concerts from all over the United States.

"Sure," Kate said, switching on her parents' old portable TV, which we always borrow for sleepovers.

". . . an incredible success story," Monty Zucco was saying when he came into focus. He's a *Video Trax* veejay, with long blond hair in a ponytail and a gold skull earring. "She started out at thirteen, singing in parking lots and shopping malls, with just a cheap cassette-player to back her up. Now, at only fifteen, she's got her own band, her own record label, her own platinum album. . . ."

"And her own Rolls Royce!" Stephanie murmured. A huge white car drove slowly up to an outdoor stage on the television screen. "I could live with that."

"She's too young to drive it," I said.

"So she pays a chauffeur to drive it for her," said Stephanie.

Sure enough, a man dressed in a black uniform

jumped out of the car, pulled open the back door, and out climbed. . . .

"Lavonne!" Monty Zucco yelled.

Big applause from the crowd.

"Ick!" said Kate, and Patti and I agreed with her. Lavonne was wearing a white sleeveless mini-dress with white lace tights and gloves. She had on pale-pink lipstick, and a white pillbox hat was perched over the poufy reddish bangs she's famous for.

"So . . . cutesy," Patti said.

"She can't even sing," I said, reaching to switch channels before Lavonne could open her mouth.

"Wait a second!" Stephanie said.

"You *like* her?" We couldn't believe it.

"For somebody who can't sing, she has a pretty good career going," Stephanie said, turning the sound down and watching Lavonne dance around the stage. "I can do that step. . . ."

Stephanie scrambled to her feet and started whirling around Kate's bedroom, imitating Lavonne exactly.

"Look out for the dip!" I snatched up the bowl just before Stephanie's foot came down on it.

"And the lamp!" Patti grabbed Kate's teetering floor lamp — Stephanie had whacked it with her arm on the way past.

20

"I've created a monster! Let's change channels before she destroys the place," Kate said grimly. She twisted the knob, switching to an old black-and-white movie.

"I was just getting going!" Stephanie panted.

"I like you better as Mavis Moore," Kate said.

"The red and black formal? Kevin DeSpain as a dinner guest?" Patti reminded her.

"You'd get sweaty from all the dancing," I said. "It would make your hair frizz." Stephanie spends a lot of time trying to make her curly hair straighter.

"All right — cooking it is," she agreed at last. "Or fashion — I'm good at that, too. Or — "

Kate stuffed a piece of super-fudge into Stephanie's mouth to quiet her, and we settled down to watch two explorers looking for a living dinosaur deep in the darkest jungle.

"Maybe they'll find Lauren's stomach," Stephanie mumbled around the fudge.

Chapter
3

Stephanie went to the city that weekend to visit her grandmother, so she couldn't bug me about talking to my mom. But I *did* talk to her, even without Stephanie pushing me. Actually, my parents talked to *me*.

"We know this job will mean quite an adjustment for you, sweetie," my mom said at a family conference in the living room on Saturday. Roger was at a track meet in Dannerville with the Riverhurst High School Team, so it was just Mom and Dad and me.

"Oh . . . uh . . . it'll be fine," I said. Then I thought of what Stephanie would say if she could hear me not sticking up for my rights. I took a deep breath. "Listen, Mom," I began. But my dad had started talking.

"We think you're being great about it," Dad said. "We just wanted to ask your opinion about a couple of things."

"Okay," I said. "Shoot."

"First of all, how would you feel if we arranged to have someone in the house with you from the time you got home from school until six?" my dad said.

"You mean like a *baby-sitter*?!" Having a baby-sitter would be a thousand times worse than spending a few hours alone in the afternoon. "I'm in the fifth grade!"

My parents both smiled. "That answers that," my dad said.

"Are you sure, Lauren?" said my mom. "What about a college student? She could also do some of the chores around the house, like vacuuming, or running a load in the washing machine."

I shook my head, hard. What would the other kids at school think if they heard I had a baby-sitter? "I'd rather do the chores myself," I said. Then I remembered Stephanie's role-playing again. "And since I'll be — "

But my mom was talking. "In that case, it's only

fair to increase your allowance. How does two dollars more a week sound?"

"Great!" I said. Nothing to it, Stephanie, I was thinking.

"Maybe we'll push your bedtime up an hour, too, to compensate for the extra time your increased responsibilities around the house will take," my dad added.

"Wow! Thanks!" I said.

"And don't think Roger won't be doing his share," my mother told me. "We'll have him busy all day on Sundays. Now — there are a few rules we'd like you to follow. First of all, I want you to call me at the office as soon as you've gotten home from school."

I nodded. "What if I want to go somewhere with Kate and the gang?"

"Then you'll have to let me know where you're going, just as you do now," said my mom.

"Also — and this is very important — please don't bring anybody into the house when there are no adults at home," my dad said. "If there were some sort of accident, if someone got hurt, it would be a very serious situation."

"Not even Stephanie and Patti and Kate?" I'd

really been counting on them to keep me company!

"Well. . . . " My mother thought it over. "I guess that would be all right, but other than heating things in the microwave, I don't want you cooking, or doing anything else that might lead to trouble. We leave it up to you to be sensible."

"I will," I promised.

"That's it, then, " Mom said. "I'll stick a short list of chores on the fridge every morning as a reminder. Remember that Mrs. Beekman will be next door, and if there are real problems, I can always drive home in about ten minutes, okay?"

"Okay," I said. Two dollars extra on my allowance and bedtime one hour later — Stephanie would be proud of me! Although I had a sneaky feeling she wouldn't really count my performance as putting my foot down.

Still, it sounded pretty impressive when I announced it to her on Monday. Every weekday morning, Stephanie and Kate and I meet on our bikes at the corner of Pine Steet and Hillcrest and wait for Patti to pedal down from her house on Mill Road. That Monday, I got there a little late because Mom wanted to give me some last-minute instructions.

Stephanie, Kate, and Patti were waiting for me.

"Did you talk to your mother?" Stephanie asked as soon as I'd braked my bike.

I nodded. "Yep."

"And?" said Stephanie.

"Two dollars more on the allowance, and an hour later for bedtime," I reported.

"Way to go, Lauren!" Stephanie exclaimed, and we slapped hands.

"That's a great sweatshirt, Stephanie," Patti said as we coasted down Hillcrest toward the school.

It wasn't her usual red, black, and white — the sweatshirt was pink, with a big sunburst, in all different colors, covering the front.

"Did you buy it in the city?" I asked.

Stephanie shook her head. "Nope. I *made* it in the city."

"You made that?" Kate turned to stare at the sweatshirt in disbelief. It really was great-looking — a giant circle of bright splashes of reds and yellows and purples, streaked with thin white lines.

"Yesterday afternoon at the museum, there was a three-hour workshop on tie-dying, and Nana and I went." Nana is Mrs. Bricker, Stephanie's grandmother. "We had to bring a bunch of rubber bands and something made of white cotton. The museum people mixed up pots of dye and showed us what to do. It's really pretty easy."

As we turned in at the bike rack in front of Riverhurst Elementary, Jane Sykes, a girl in 5B with us, called out, "Hey, Stephanie — I love your sweatshirt!"

"Did you get it at the mall?" asked Tracy Osner from 5A.

"No, actually, I made it," Stephanie replied.

"Wow!" Tracy said admiringly. "Could you make one for me? I'll pay you!"

"Well. . . ." Stephanie shrugged. "I *guess* so."

"Would five dollars be okay?" Tracy asked.

"I'd like one, too," Jane Sykes said.

"And me!" Sally Mason piped up — she's also in 5B. "And one for my cousin Melanie — it's her birthday next week."

Four sweatshirts at five dollars apiece . . . Stephanie had made twenty dollars in a couple of minutes!

"Okay — you'll have to bring me white, one-hundred-percent cotton sweatshirts in the right sizes," Stephanie said.

"I'll give you mine tomorrow," Sally told her. "I'd like the background of mine to be blue, okay? With yellow and red in the circle. And my cousin's to be green."

Jane wanted pink, and Tracy asked for yellow. "And we'll have the money for you in the morning, too," Jane said.

"It sounds like we're in business," said Stephanie.

Between the time the first bell rang to go into the school building and the second bell rang for class to start, Stephanie got four more orders, three of them from guys in our class: Mark Freedman, Larry Jackson, and Henry Larkin.

Stephanie's desk is in the front row in 5B, and Kate and I sit right behind her. "Cooking or fashion?" she murmured to us as she scribbled down orders in her notebook. "I think I'll just have to try them both, and whichever I'm best at, *wins*."

"And what if you're *fabulous* at them both," Kate whispered back, raising an eyebrow at me.

"Then I won't have to limit myself, will I?" Stephanie answered.

When Stephanie puts her mind to something, there's no stopping her!

Chapter
4

When school was over that afternoon, I took so long to load my books into my backpack that by the time I'd finished, everyone in 5B had cleared out except Kate, Patti, and Stephanie. Then I lagged so far behind on the way down the front walk that Kate finally complained. "Lauren, are you wearing cement sneakers?"

The truth was, I wasn't looking forward to going home. Before, when I knew Mom had an appointment at the dentist in the afternoon, or she was going to be out shopping or something, I sort of enjoyed having the house to myself for a few hours. I could hang out, play music as loud as I wanted, that kind of thing. But knowing that I'd have it to myself every

29

day from now on, from three-thirty till dinner, was a lot less attractive.

Sure, I had some chores to do — I was supposed to fold up the clean towels in the dryer, set the table, and heat up the spaghetti sauce Mom had made the night before. But chores certainly weren't going to fill the two-and-a-half hours until the rest of my family got home. I *could* go over to Kate's, but I didn't want the Beekmans to get sick of looking at me so soon.

I was really feeling kind of sorry for myself when Kate said, "Why don't we all go over to Lauren's and keep her company for a while?"

"Good idea," Patti said.

"Stephanie?" said Kate.

But Stephanie had stopped about ten feet from the bike rack, next to a noisy group of boys. She put her finger to her lips for a second and then fumbled with her tote bag, pretending she was looking for something. She was eavesdropping on what the guys were saying.

Mark Freedman was the only fifth-grader in the bunch. The others were all sixth-graders: Matthew Yates, Andy Hersh — his sister, Nancy, is in 5B — and Taylor Sprouse, who thinks he's the coolest guy in school. Taylor was wearing a black sweatshirt with a big hole in the elbow, black jeans, black hightops, and a silver dog chain wrapped around his wrist. He kept flipping his straight, light-brown hair out of his eyes with a jerk of his head.

"We're leaving!" Kate mouthed to Stephanie as we pulled our bikes out of the rack.

Stephanie frowned at Kate, but she strolled over to us and strapped her tote to the black-and-red fifteen speed.

"What were they talking about?" Patti asked.

"They're starting a band," Stephanie answered. "Mark'll be the drummer. Andy Hersh will play electric keyboard. . . ."

"And Taylor?" I wanted to know.

"Lead guitar," Stephanie said.

"Natch," said Kate.

"They're going to call themselves Fresh," Stephanie reported, "and they're going to try for gigs at parties, and school dances."

"Look at Jenny drooling all over Taylor!" Kate said. "Do you think she has any idea how ridiculous she looks?"

Jenny Carlin's in our class, too. She's absolutely boy-crazy.

"I don't ever like to agree with Jenny, but I have

31

to admit, Taylor Sprouse is really good-looking,"
Stephanie said. "I wonder if Fresh needs a girl
singer?" she added thoughtfully.

"You can't sing," Kate said.

"Neither can Lavonne," Stephanie said, "but
that hasn't slowed *her* down any."

"Come on, Stephanie," Kate said. "This morning it was cooking or fashion. Now it's singing in a
band. Where will it end?"

"Good thing we don't have to stick to what we
pick now," Patti put in. "My mom told me once that
when she was my age, she really wanted to be a
rodeo cowgirl."

Patti's mother on a bucking bronco was a pretty
funny idea. We were all giggling as we pedaled up
Hillcrest to Pine Street. But I could tell Stephanie was
taking this career idea a little more seriously.

It was kind of weird finding the house locked
up tight, as though my whole family had gone on
vacation without me. Bullwinkle was on guard in the
backyard — which is a total joke. Bullwinkle just
might knock a stranger down, but only so that he
could lick the stranger's face better.

I pulled out my new set of house keys and let
us into the kitchen.

"What time is it?" Stephanie asked as soon as we'd taken our jackets off.

Kate looked at her watch. "Three thirty-five."

"Quick — Mavis Moore's on!" Stephanie said.

She rushed into the den and switched on the TV. Mavis was talking to a small, thin man dressed in a white jacket, pants, and apron, with a tall chef's hat on his head.

". . . is Louis Lavalle, from Chez" (Mavis pronounced it "Shay") "Lavalle, who is here with us today to prepare his specialty, tripe with carrots and onions."

"What's tripe?" I asked, sitting down on the couch between Kate and Stephanie.

They shook their heads.

"Who knows?" Stephanie said. "Isn't Mavis wearing a great outfit?" Mavis Moore had on a long, dark-red plaid skirt with a matching shawl, a black turtleneck sweater, and gold hoop earrings.

"Where's your dictionary, Lauren?" Patti asked. She's really into looking things up, which is why her vocabulary is so much better than the rest of ours.

"Somewhere in my room — maybe in the closet?" I said without thinking.

"Be right back," Patti said.

Mavis was beaming at Chef Lavalle as he turned

to a table behind him for a plate of something grayish-white.

"It looks sort of like a honeycomb," Stephanie said when he picked up a piece of the stuff and held it toward the camera.

"More like a worn-out bath sponge," said Kate.

"I 'ave simmaired ze tripe for sree-and-a-half hours, until eet ees tendair," Chef Lavalle said.

"A rubber tire would be tender if you simmered it for three-and-a-half hours," Kate murmured.

"I cut eet op, lak so." He used scissors to cut the sponge into strips. "Zen I put eet into a pot weez canned tomatoes, paipper, carrots, on-nions, celery, and 'alf a cup of boiled 'am, wan pound mush-rooms," Chef Lavalle went on. "I covair . . ."

There was a crash over our heads!

"Oh, wow! I forgot — I crammed a bunch of stuff into my closet this morning!" I jumped off the couch and dashed into the front hall. "Patti — are you all right?" I yelled up the stairs.

"Fine," she called back. "I'm afraid I've made kind of a mess up here, though."

"No, I made the mess," I said. "Did you find the dictionary?"

"Yes — it was in the closet. I'll be down in a second."

By the time Patti got back to the den, Mavis Moore and her guests — a bald actor from England named Roddy Barnett and an old duchess from Spain in a shiny green dress — had sat down to eat. The table was set with gold-rimmed plates, lots of silverware and candles, and a flower arrangement.

"So, did you find out what tripe is?" Kate asked Patti as Mavis and the actor dug in.

"Yes," Patti said. "Tripe is the inside of a cow's stomach."

"YUCK!" Everybody screeched at once.

We switched off Mavis pretty fast. Still, it would take more than cows' stomachs to ruin *our* appetites. Mom had bought a week's worth of munchies on Saturday, so Kate and Stephanie and Patti and I dug in.

We watched *Video Trax* for a while, and Stephanie practiced some steps to the music. Then I figured I should get dinner started. Kate went down to the basement to fold the towels in the dryer, and Patti started setting the table for dinner — she knows how to make fancy designs with the napkins.

"I'll help you cook," Stephanie offered.

"All I really have to do is heat up the spaghetti sauce," I said.

"Let me try it first." Stephanie stuck her finger

into the pot of sauce and touched it to her tongue. She shook her head. "Not really tasty enough, do you think? I had some great sauce at Perillo's in the city on Saturday. It had black and green olives in it, parsley, some anchovies. . . ."

"Roger doesn't eat fish," I said. Actually, it's more than that. Roger doesn't eat fish because he's allergic to it — it gives him a really gruesome rash.

But Stephanie wasn't paying much attention. She opened the refrigerator and checked out the little jars and bottles on the inside of the door. "Hey — you've got some green olives, and here are some black ones, too. . . ."

"Lauren, do you want to help me carry these towels upstairs?" Kate yelled from the basement.

"Sure," I shouted down to her. "Not *too* tasty," I warned Stephanie as she unscrewed the top on a jar of green olives. "Remember the chili?"

While Stephanie fiddled with the sauce, Kate and I carried two armloads each of towels up to the second floor and put them away in the linen closet in the hall. We were headed downstairs again when Kate glanced into my room. "Lauren — I can't believe it! You've cleaned up!" she exclaimed.

"Cleaned up?" I peered through the door, too.

The floor was clear, not littered with books and clothes and shoes the way it usually is. The shelves in the bookcases against the wall were neatly arranged, not crammed with copies of *Confidentially Yours* and *Star Turns*, old homework papers, or clean socks that hadn't quite made it to my chest-of-drawers yet. The bedspreads had been smoothed out, the pillows fluffed up. Even Rocky, my black-and-white kitten, looked spiffier than usual, sleeping in a tidy ball on the chair instead of sprawled all over the place.

My dictionary was lying in the exact center of my desk. "Patti did it," I said to Kate. "She probably jammed all the mess into the closet."

But the closet was organized, too!

"Where's your camera?" Kate teased. "I want to get a picture of this — it's a once-in-a-lifetime opportunity!"

Patti stuck her head into my room about then. "I hope you don't mind, Lauren, " she said shyly. "After I picked up the stuff I'd spilled out of your closet, I was on a roll, and — "

"Are you kidding?" I replied. "My room hasn't looked this good since . . . since . . ."

"Since before you could walk, 'cause you

couldn't reach anything to mess it up," Kate finished with a grin. She checked her watch. "It's after five — I'd better get home."

"Me, too," Patti said. "I have to do a project for the Quarks meeting." Patti belongs to Quarks, a science club for very smart kids.

Stephanie was just taking the sauce out of the microwave when we walked back into the kitchen. She held out a spoonful. "What about this?" she said.

"Excellent!" I answered as soon as I'd swallowed. "I can see the olives, but what else is in here?"

"Secrets of Chef Green." Stephanie flashed a smile for the imaginary TV cameras. "I guess it's time to hit the trail," she said to Kate and Patti.

"Thanks, guys, for keeping me company," I said, "and for helping me with the chores." It looked like having my mom in an office wasn't going to be so bad after all.

And were Mom and Dad impressed when they got home!

"The table looks beautiful," my mother said as she filled a big pot of water to boil the spaghetti. "Did you remember to fold the towels and put them away?"

"Not only did she put away the towels" — Dad had already zoomed upstairs to change into his jeans — "but wait until you see her room, Ann!" he called from the front hall. "You've certainly been busy, sweetie," Dad said to me.

"Oh . . ." I shrugged my shoulders as if it were nothing, meanwhile thinking maybe they'd raise my allowance again soon, or let me stay up even later.

Everything was fine until Roger got home from practice and all four of us sat down to dinner. Mom served the spaghetti, ladled the sauce onto it, and passed the grated cheese around.

"This sauce is terrific!" my dad said to my mom after his first bite. "Compliments to the cook!"

"Mmm! It is good," Mom said, "but I'm afraid I can't take all the credit. What else did you add besides olives, Lauren?"

I couldn't really answer that, since Chef Green hadn't revealed her secret to me. I happened to glance at my dad and noticed he was looking at my brother. Naturally, I looked, too.

Roger had been eating the whole time the rest of us were talking, scarfing down the spaghetti and sauce like there was no tomorrow. And suddenly I was pretty certain about one of the mystery ingredients at least — *anchovies!*

Roger's face was absolutely covered with bright red blotches the size of dimes!

Chapter 5

"I told you about Roger and fish, Stephanie!" I said the next morning as we pedaled toward school. "You just weren't listening."

"I was listening!" Stephanie protested. "You said, 'Roger doesn't eat fish,' not 'Roger can't eat fish.' So I thought he'd gotten some dumb idea that he didn't *like* fish. And I knew that he wouldn't be able to see the anchovies in the sauce, because they're cut into such little bits. And I figured what he couldn't see wouldn't bother him."

It was another case of Stephanie thinking she knows best. Even if it *had* been that Roger just didn't like fish, why should he have to eat it if he didn't want to? But I kept my mouth shut.

"Actually, he liked the sauce," I told her. "A

lot. He ate a ton of it really fast. Then all at once he started to break out in these enormous blotches. . . ."
I had to giggle, remembering, "Like giant chicken pox."

"Was he mad?" Kate wanted to know.

"Furious! He yelled that I was trying to poison him. He was supposed to have a study date with Linda last night" — Linda is Roger's girlfriend — "but the madder he got, the blotchier his face got. He had to cancel the date."

"Is he all right now?" Patti asked.

I nodded. "He took an allergy pill, and the spots started to fade in a couple of hours. He was back to normal this morning."

"'You didn't get into trouble, did you?" Stephanie sounded a little guilty.

"Not really. But Mom said from now on we have to clear it with her before we add anything else to food that she's cooked," I said.

The four of us jumped our bikes onto the sidewalk in front of Riverhurst Elementary, and turned off at the bike rack. Right away, we were surrounded by Stephanie's customers, all with their white, one-hundred-percent-cotton sweatshirts: Sally with three and Jane, Tracy, Tracy's little sister, Lisa, Mark, Henry, Larry one each. By the time we got to class,

41

we were carrying ten white sweatshirts between us, and Stephanie had a lot of money in her pocket.

There was just one problem. "Most of the kids want their orders back right away," Stephanie said as we headed into the building. "Do you guys think you could help me with them?"

"It sounds like fun," Patti said.

"Great! We can start this afternoon at my house." said Stephanie.

I shook my head. "I can't — I have to be at home, because Slumbertown is delivering my parents' new mattress between three-thirty and six."

"Then we'll do it at your house!" Stephanie said. "'You have that big sink in the basement. We can spread out down there, without having to worry that we're going to mess up the rest of the house."

"Just how messy is this?" Kate asked. "I don't particularly want to stand around with my hands in glop."

"It's not glop," Stephanie told her. "It's more like Easter egg dye. And we can do some T-shirts for ourselves, too. My dad has twelve brand-new ones, still in their wrappers. He won't mind if I take four for us. Okay?"

Kate shrugged. "Are you sure it's all right, Lauren?"

"We wouldn't want you to get in any more trouble," Patti said.

"I guess so," I answered. "As long as we stay out of the kitchen." I didn't want Stephanie anywhere near the meatloaf we'd be having for dinner that evening.

Stephanie held up her right hand. "I promise."

When school was over that day, Kate and I biked straight to my house with the sweatshirts. Patti and Stephanie rode on down Pine Street to the Greens' to pick up the dye, a king-size box of rubber bands, and some string. They also nabbed four of Mr. Green's new T-shirts for the Sleepover Friends.

As soon as they'd gotten back, the four of us dug out all the smaller buckets and larger mixing bowls we could find, and hauled them down to the basement.

There was a big pile of white wash — mostly sheets — beside the washing machine. "I'm supposed to do this load of laundry before Mom gets home," I said to Kate. "Don't let me forget."

"You'd better get it out of the way," Kate said. "You don't want to drip dye on it."

"Especially not on Roger's favorite white shirt," I said, pointing at a long sleeve sticking out of the

43

side of the pile. I moved the white wash over near the stairs.

"First we fill up the containers with water," Stephanie told us, "and then we mix in the dye." She'd brought large packages of red and blue and yellow dye, and smaller ones of pink and neon green and scarlet. "Is there another light we can turn on, Lauren?"

"Only that one bulb over the washer," I replied. "The one above the stairs doesn't work."

Stephanie shrugged. "Okay — over to the sink."

We filled up the bowls and buckets and stood them around on the basement floor. Then we tore open the packages of dye and started adding the colored powder to the water.

"Wow — this scarlet is a wonderful color!" Patti said, twirling it around with her hand to mix it. Then she took her hand out of the bowl and stared at it. It was flaming scarlet to the wrist!

"Oh — I guess we should be using something besides our hands to do the stirring," Stephanie said.

"Good thought," said Kate, climbing the stairs for spoons.

Pretty soon we had eight containers of dye

ready: two red, two blue, and one each of the other colors.

Then Stephanie assigned us one sweatshirt apiece. I got Tracy's. "It's the medium with a tag that says 'R.A.P.' " Stephanie peered at her list under the light. "Tracy wanted a yellow background, and she left the colors in the center up to us."

Kate was doing Henry Larkin's; Patti, Jane Sykes'; and Stephanie would demonstrate on Mark Freedman's.

"To start off, you have to get the sweatshirts completely wet," Stephanie said, holding Mark's under the faucet in the sink. "Then wring it out until you can't squeeze out another drop of water."

She waited until Kate and Patti and I had followed her instructions.

"Okay, everybody knows about colors, right? Like red and blue make purple, and red and yellow make orange, and yellow and blue make green?"

We all nodded.

"Then you know what should mix and what shouldn't. For instance, if your sweatshirt is supposed to have a pink background, like Jane's is, you'll dip the whole thing in pink dye first. Then you can dip only little pieces of the center of the shirt in the darker dyes. Understand? Otherwise, the pink will disappear under the darker colors."

It was more complicated than it looked, but it was neat! In order to get the thin, spider-webby white lines, I wrapped little puckers of sweatshirt around and around with rubber bands. I made white stripes on the arms by tying them with string.

Then I dipped the whole sweatshirt a few times in the bucket of yellow dye. After I'd let it drip for a while over the sink, I dunked each of the rubber-banded puckers in a different color: red, blue, scarlet, neon green.

"We'll stick them in the dryer to speed things up," Stephanie said.

We turned the dryer to "high" and set it for fifteen minutes. While it ran, we munched on cheese dip and sourcream potato chips and drank Dr Pepper in the kitchen. Then we rushed back down to the basement and took the sweatshirts out of the dryer. We pulled off the rubber bands and string. . . .

"This one is terrific!" I exclaimed, holding up Tracy's. "I wish it were mine!" It looked like sunshine and part of a rainbow.

"I love Jane's, too," Patti said, admiring her work.

Even Kate had to admit that the sweatshirts we'd tie-dyed were fantastic.

"Let's do ours now," I suggested.

"Can't we please finish the orders first?" Stephanie said. "I'd rather get them out of the way, and then make extra-special shirts for us."

I was wrapping rubber bands around Larry Jackson's sweatshirt when suddenly there was an outburst from Bullwinkle in the backyard.

"I forgot about my parents' new mattress," I groaned. "Bullwinkle's probably knocked the deliverymen flat!"

I dropped the sweatshirt on the washer and raced for the stairs.

"Look out!" Stephanie screeched. But the light was dim, and my right sneaker had already connected with a bucket full of red dye. It sailed into the air like a soccer ball . . . and dumped dye for yards!

"Oh, no! Mom is going to kill me!" I picked up the bucket, but it was almost completely empty. Most of the dye had settled on the pile of white wash.

"We'll deal with this, Lauren," Kate said.

"You better go call off Bullwinkle," Patti added.

Sure enough, Bullwinkle had the guys from

Slumbertown squashed between my parents' new mattress and the back fence.

"He won't bite!" I called to them as I dashed out the back door.

"Maybe not, but he's about to drown me!" spluttered one man as Bullwinkle licked his face.

By the time I'd locked the dog in the garage, shown the deliverymen where to put the new mattress, and led them downstairs with the old mattress, Kate, Patti, and Stephanie were out of the basement.

"Sorry to leave you with a mess, Lauren, but it's almost five-thirty," Kate told me. "I have to get home, because we're going out to dinner."

"I do, too — my parents are having the head of the history department over tonight," Patti said. "We did clean up the floor, though, and we poured out the rest of the dye. Only the bowls and buckets are left."

"I'm taking the sweatshirts and everything else home with me," Stephanie added.

"The white wash?" I wasn't sure I really wanted to know.

"Most of the dye hit the dish towels on top of the pile," Kate said. "Your mom probably won't mind that too much."

"And Roger's shirt?" I asked.

"One red arm," Patti answered.

"Actually, it looks sort of cool," Stephanie said.

I had a strong feeling that Roger wouldn't agree with her.

As soon as the three of them had left, I hurried back down to the basement. I crammed the white — and red — wash into the machine, turned it on, and added detergent and quarts of bleach.

And it worked, sort of. Most of the spots of dye faded completely . . . but not Roger's sleeve. When I took his shirt out of the washer, it no longer had a cool-looking red sleeve. Instead, it had a sick-looking pink one.

Chapter 6

Not as sick as Roger looked when he saw it, though.

"Where's my white shirt, Mom?" he said as soon as he got home. "I want to wear it tonight."

"What about your dinner?" said Mom.

"Linda and I are going out for pizza," Roger said.

"Lauren, did you do the white wash I left in the basement?" Mom asked me.

"Er . . . yes," I mumbled. "It's . . . uh . . . in the dryer."

Roger was all the way down the basement stairs before I had time to say anything else. I heard him open the dryer. It was quiet while he dug around in the other white stuff. And then. . . . "*Aaargh!*"

"Roger, is everything okay down there?" Mom called out.

"NO! She's wrecked it!" he roared.

"Wrecked what?" my mother said, eyeing me.

"MY SHIRT!" Roger came pounding up the stairs, waving it in front of him. "Do you know how much this shirt cost me?" he shouted at me. "Most of my birthday money! Look at this!" He shook the pink sleeve at Mom.

"Oh, dear, Lauren, how on earth did that happen?" Mom said.

"I'm really sorry," I said. "We were helping Stephanie out with some tie-dyeing in the basement, and Bullwinkle started barking at the mattress guys, and on the way to the stairs I knocked over a bucket of red dye. . . ."

"I knew it — she's out to get me!" Roger yelled. "First she poisons me with anchovies, and now she ruins my *favorite* shirt!"

"I'm sure Lauren will be happy to buy you another one, Roger," my mom said, studying me. "You can get one this weekend at the mall. I'll pay for it, and Lauren will pay me back out of her allowance."

The shirt was imported from Italy, and I was

51

pretty sure I remembered what it had cost — over forty dollars! I'd be paying for it for months! But fair is fair, I guess.

"Well . . . okay." Roger scowled at me one last time and stomped off to his room.

Mom shook her head and sighed. "Lauren, you've only been alone for two afternoons so far, and there have been problems both times."

"I'm sorry, Mom. I didn't mean to cause any. . . ."

"I know you didn't, sweetie," my mother said. "And I know that Stephanie was just trying to help you out with dinner, and that you were trying to help her out with her tie-dyeing. But, Lauren, you're in charge of the house now. If you think there might be problems when one of your friends suggests something, you're going to have to learn to say no. It's difficult, but you'll find that it saves you a lot of trouble in the long run."

I couldn't believe my ears. First I get a pep talk from Stephanie about putting my foot down with my parents. And now my mom was telling me to learn to say no to Stephanie.

When I thought about it, though, it wasn't hard to decide who had taken more advantage of me. Who had raised my allowance without even being asked? Mom and Dad. And who had *cost* me my allowance for weeks, and gotten me into trouble with my brother? Not my parents — Stephanie!

Still, when she asked me the next day about using our garage, I just couldn't seem to say no.

Stephanie brought the four sweatshirts we'd dyed to school that morning, and she got seven more orders without even trying.

"Christy Soames, Betsy Chalfin, Karen Sims. . . ." She sat down on the front steps of Riverhurst Elementary to scribble the names in her notebook. Next she checked off a few: "I gave Tracy her sweatshirt, and Jane. . . . Oh — there's Mark."

Mark Freedman, Andy Hersh, Matthew Yates, and Taylor Sprouse were standing in a huddle near the bus stop, looking very serious.

Stephanie scrambled to her feet and waltzed over to them to present Mark with his sweatshirt.

"Sixth-grade boys and a fifth-grade girl?" Kate said to Patti and me. "I'll bet you a lime freeze at Charlie's that they snub her."

If we had taken Kate up on it, she would have lost. They were too far away for us to hear the conversation, but we could tell that first Stephanie said something, and then Mark, and then Stephanie again, and then Taylor Sprouse.

He talked for so long that the first bell rang and he still wasn't finished.

We waved to Stephanie to come on, but she was listening to Taylor.

"I'm not going to spend my lunch hour with Mrs. Wainwright just so Stephanie can hang on that fathead's every word," Kate said. Mrs. Wainwright is our principal. If you're late more than once, you have to sit in her office during lunch. We'd spent one miserable lunch period there — and once was enough.

"I'm not either," said Patti.

"What could he possibly be saying all this time?" I wondered as we walked into the school building.

"He's talking about his favorite topic," Kate guessed. *"Himself."*

Stephanie made it to class with just about twenty seconds before the late bell. She rushed through the door and dropped into her seat without turning around.

"What's up?" Kate whispered in her left ear.

Stephanie shook her head. "Tell you at lunch," she whispered over her shoulder.

"Class, get out your math homework," said Mrs. Mead.

Math, then science, then social studies, then reading.

Then out to the cafeteria for franks and beans. As soon as Kate and Patti and Stephanie and I had plunked our trays down at our regular table, Kate said, "Okay, Stephanie — give. What was the big powwow at the bus stop all about?"

Stephanie took a bite of her frankfurter and chewed for a while. "The band's in trouble," she said at last.

"What kind of trouble?" Patti asked.

"They don't have a place to practice anymore." Stephanie replied. "They used to play at Mark's in the basement, but his grandmother is visiting for a while, and the music gives her a migraine."

"What about Andy's?" Kate asked.

"Too many little kids around." There are five children in the Hersh family.

"Matthew?" I said.

"His mother hates rock and roll," Stephanie answered.

"And Mr. Cool?" said Kate.

"Taylor? His neighbors are totally uncool — they complain all the time," Stephanie said. "His

55

parents are going to soundproof the den, but it will take a few weeks."

"Mark's a nice guy, but it isn't our problem, " Kate said.

"Well, actually, it kind of *is*," Stephanie said, looking at us out of the corner of her eye.

"What's that supposed to mean?" Kate wanted to know.

"Well . . . Fresh would consider having a girl singer *if* they could find a place to practice." Stephanie pushed the beans around on her plate.

"Like you?" Kate snorted. "Are you still thinking about being the next Lavonne?"

"But we can't practice at my house. My mom says she wants as much quiet as possible until the baby comes," Stephanie said, ignoring Kate's remarks.

"Mine's out, too," said Patti. "I've got Quarks this afternoon."

"Not my house!" Kate said firmly. "My dad keeps odd hours, and I don't think he wants to follow a long shift in the emergency room with a concert by Fresh."

"Actually, I was thinking of Lauren's," Stephanie said, looking directly at me for the first time since we'd sat down.

"No way," I said. "My parents don't want anyone in the house when Mom's at work. Except us, of course." There — that was easy enough.

"Not the house," Stephanie said. "The garage."

"Our *garage?*" I was too surprised to come up with an instant argument.

"It'd be perfect!" Stephanie said enthusiastically. "It's got plenty of windows for light. It has to have electricity, because your dad uses his power tools out there — we'll need electricity for the piano and guitars. We can slide the doors closed, so we won't disturb anybody. And we'll leave before your parents get home. Please, Lauren? Please. . . ."

I honestly couldn't think of a good enough reason to say no. "Well, I . . . ," I began.

"Thanks!" Stephanie squealed. She bounced out of her chair and hurried across the cafeteria to give Mark and Taylor and the others the good news.

"Lauren . . ." Patti began, but she didn't seem to know what else to say.

Kate sighed and rolled her eyes at me. "Sometimes you amaze me, Lauren," she said.

Chapter
7

When I called Mom that afternoon, I didn't really lie. I told her that I was home from school, and that I was alone in the house, both of which were true.

The backyard, though, was a different story. Mrs. Sprouse, who seems to spend her entire life doing everything Taylor tells her to, had just pulled into the driveway in a green van. As soon as she'd stopped, the back doors of the van swung out, and the band started unloading next to the garage: drums, guitars, a keyboard, speakers, miles of extension cord, even a couple of microphones. It looked like the display window at Main Street Music!

I walked outside and slid open the big wooden doors of the garage for them.

"Hey, Lauren!" Mark Freeman said. "It's great that you're letting us practice here."

"Yeah — thanks," Andy and Matthew said.

"We were beginning to think we were out of luck," Andy added.

"It's just until I get my sound-proof studio," Taylor reminded them. "Right, Mom?"

"That's right, dear," said Mrs. Sprouse. She's a small woman, but she picked up a big speaker and lugged it toward the garage.

Taylor nodded coolly at me before turning back to the other guys, "Let's not waste any more time!"

Stephanie rode up on her bike about then. She'd gone home to change into an all-black outfit. It was probably to make points with Taylor, although on the way home she'd told us, "You know how Lavonne wears all white? Well, I'm going to wear all black."

Taylor put her to work right away, hauling equipment. Then he moved out of the line of traffic himself, and fiddled with his guitar strings while he stared into space.

"He is the worst!" a voice hissed from behind me — I was standing just outside the garage.

I jumped, but it was only Kate. She'd taken the

59

shortcut to my house through the hedges and Donald Foster's backyard.

"I didn't think you were coming over today," I said. When school was out that afternoon, Patti had gone to her usual Wednesday science club meeting, and Kate had muttered something about having to help her mother.

"My curiosity got the best of me," Kate replied. "Is he for *real*?"

Mark, Andy, Matthew, Stephanie, and Mrs. Sprouse were scurrying around like ants, lifting, carrying, and arranging. But Taylor was slouched in a corner, eyes closed, lips barely moving, plunking silently away on his unplugged guitar.

He looked so *full of himself*! Kate and I started to giggle. Taylor's eyes flew open, and he glared at us. Not for more than a second, though — we probably weren't worth the effort.

"I think we're finished, Taylor," Mrs. Sprouse announced brightly. "When would you like me to come back for you?"

"Five-thirty," Taylor said. "Ready, guys?" he added, dismissing his mother. As she climbed into the van, he reached down and plugged in his guitar. "Let's start with 'Break It Up.' On three: one . . . two . . ."

"Taylor!" Stephanie called out. "What about me?"

"Oh. Yeah. Do you think you could get us something to drink?" he said.

"I mean about my singing," said Stephanie.

Taylor frowned. "We'll practice the instrumentals first," he said. "Are Cokes okay, guys?" he asked Andy and the others.

"Sure."

"Cokes . . . uh . . . Stephanie," Taylor said.

"He barely remembers her name," Kate murmured to me.

"Then why did he want her for a singer?" I wondered.

"You could have been the singer, or me, or anybody who'd find him a place to practice," Kate said.

"Is that all right?" Stephanie asked me, stopping outside the garage. "About the Cokes and stuff."

"I guess so." At this rate, I was thinking, the munchies Mom bought will never last till the weekend.

Taylor began again. "One . . . two . . . three!"

On *three*, there was the most incredible noise — kind of like a car crash! Half the dogs in the neighborhood started barking their heads off. Bullwinkle howled at the top of his lungs — he was locked in the house, in the spare room upstairs.

"Close 'em!" Kate yelled. She ran for one of the wooden garage doors, and I grabbed the other. We pushed hard, and they slid together, right before the next chord from Fresh. The doors muffled the sound, at least a little.

"They're really good, aren't they?" Stephanie said to Kate and me over a drum roll from Mark.

Kate sniffed. "I think I'll go see if Mavis is having tripe again," she said, heading for the house.

We followed Kate in. Stephanie opened the refrigerator and took out a king-sized Coke. "Fill five glasses with ice, okay, Lauren?" she said. "Isn't this terrific? I can just see the album jacket: 'Stephanie, with Fresh!' Look out, Lavonne, here I come!"

Stephanie poured Coke into the glasses, loaded them onto Mom's best tray, grabbed a bag of taco-flavored corn chips out of the cabinet, and shot out the back door. Then she opened it again, just a crack. "Thanks a lot, Lauren, for helping me out. You'll get my first gold record for your bedroom wall!" The door clicked behind her.

Twang! Another chord from Fresh. Even with the garage closed up tight, I could hear it clearly. I wondered about the Martins across the street — was it setting their teeth on edge? Or Mr. Winkler, who's getting old and kind of cranky? Or the Norrises at the end of the street — Mrs. Norris is a little jumpy — or Donald's mom or even the Beekmans?

Suddenly there was a knock at the front door.

"Who's that?" Kate called from the den.

"Probably somebody coming to complain," I groaned.

But it wasn't. It was a little boy about four or five years old. "Who are you?" he said when I opened the door.

"Lauren Hunter. Who are you?"

"Brian Hersh. I'm supposed to stay with my brother while my mom's at the doctor," he said.

"Wonderful — now we're baby-sitters," Kate said. She'd come to the door when she heard Brian's voice.

"Where's Andy?" Brian asked suspiciously.

"He's in the garage, Brian, practicing. I'll take you to him right now," I said.

"Wait a second — look who's coming down the street," Kate said to me. She pointed at two girls on bicycles, pedaling slowly down Pine.

"Jenny Carlin!" I said.

"And Angela," said Kate. Angela Kemp is Jenny's faithful sidekick.

"Where could they be going?" Pine is a dead-end street, and I couldn't think of a single person that Jenny might want to visit.

"Here, of course," said Kate.

"Here!" Jenny Carlin can't stand any of the Sleepover Friends, but she especially can't stand me.

At the beginning of the year, Jenny decided she liked Pete Stone, a boy in 5B. Then, for some reason, Pete Stone got interested in me. Jenny thinks everyone is as boy-crazy as she is, and she was sure I had set out to make Pete Stone like me more than he liked her. And she's never forgiven me for it, even though he's changed his mind about a hundred times since then.

"Jenny's like a bloodhound, on the trail of Taylor Sprouse," Kate murmured.

Jenny and Angela had braked their bikes a little past my house, on the opposite side of the street. Now they seemed to be listening — their noses were kind of raised in the air, too.

I giggled. "Jenny does look like she's sniffing the wind for a scent."

Sproing! Fresh again. Jenny and Angela turned their bikes around and pedaled straight up my driveway!

"I don't want Jenny Carlin in my yard!" I protested to Kate.

"Don't tell me — tell her. Better yet, tell Stephanie to find someplace else to practice," Kate advised, giving me a hard look.

"I can't! I don't want to make a scene." I said.

Kate shook her head. "There's a really old movie on Channel twenty-one," she said, walking back to the den. "If you need me, you know where to find me."

"Let's go see Andy, Brian," I said absently. I was watching Jenny and Angela as they propped their bikes against my hedge and followed the noise to the garage. I reached down for the little boy's hand. "Brian?" Then I looked down — no Brian.

"Kate — is Brian with you?" I called out.

"Nope," she answered. "He probably got tired of waiting and went out to the garage by himself."

"I'd better make sure," I said, heading for the kitchen door.

Chapter
8

As soon as I stepped out onto the back porch, I could see that Jenny and Angela weren't the only unwanted visitors at 11 Pine Street. There were some sixth-graders I hardly knew hanging around outside my garage — Taylor must have invited them. And there were a few that I knew all too well, like Wendy Rodwin, Mary Seaford, and a couple of their snobby friends. When I walked past them, not one of them even smiled at me. I was a stranger in my own backyard!

The garage doors were open a foot or so, and the twangs and bangs and sproings were coming fast and furious. Andy was bobbing and weaving at the keyboard; Mark was beating up his drums. Matthew and Taylor were pretending to be rock stars, twisting around and jumping up and down while they played a lot of fast stuff on their electric guitars.

Jenny and Angela had squeezed into a corner near my dad's power tools. Stephanie was standing in another corner, still waiting to sing.

I was closing the doors behind me, trying to keep some of the noise inside, when Taylor shouted, "Hey! Leave the doors alone — it's hot in here!"

The rest of the band kept playing, but he stomped over to a window and pushed it all the way up. Then he pushed up another one. There were cheers from the audience in the yard as Fresh poured through the windows.

I picked my way over the extension cords to close the nearest window with a bang.

Stephanie rushed over to me. "Lauren!" she yelled over the music. "You're going to make Taylor mad!"

"Taylor is making *me* mad!" I yelled back. "My garage has been taken over by a guy who enjoys being rude! He's probably going to get me into trouble with his noise, my yard is full of people I don't even like — "

"You'll mess this up for me if you don't stop it

right now!" Stephanie said as I slammed down a second window.

"Stephanie, has he let you sing yet?" I asked her.

"Um . . . not yet," Stephanie replied. "They like to practice the instrumentals first."

"First, last, and always," I said. "Taylor needed a place to practice, and you found him one. He's not interested in having a girl singer. He isn't interested in anyone being a star but himself!"

"That's not true!" Stephanie said sharply.

Meanwhile, Taylor had made his way over to the doors and pushed them all the way open. Fresh was booming out of the garage, and up and down Pine Street!

"That does it!" I reached for the nearest extension cord and pulled it out of the wall. Andy's keyboard quit working.

"Lauren!" Stephanie shrieked.

I yanked out another cord. Taylor's guitar died, mid-note.

Mark frowned and stopped playing. Matthew did, too.

"Now what?" Taylor growled at me.

"Practice is over," I said.

But it wasn't over soon enough. Through the

open garage doors, I saw a green-and-white police car rolling slowly up my driveway!

Jenny and Angela were out of the garage and on their bikes in a flash. Wendy and Mary Seaford and the other sixth-graders started inching their way toward the alley.

Even Taylor looked nervous, although he tried to cover it up by jerking his head a few times to flip his hair out of his eyes.

Officer Warner got out of the car and strolled toward us. "Hello, Lauren," he said when he saw me. "We've had a couple of complaints about noise over here."

My knees were feeling kind of wobbly. My first week in charge, and I was already in trouble with the law! "It won't happen again," I said, hoping I sounded sincere enough.

Officer Warner took a closer look at Taylor. "You're the Sprouse boy, aren't you?"

"Uh . . . yes . . . yes, sir," Taylor fumbled.

"I think I've called on you in your own neighborhood for the same kind of problem, haven't I?"

"Y-yes, sir," Taylor stammered. Definitely uncool.

"I hope I won't have to speak to you about it again," Officer Warner said.

"No, sir."

Office Warner nodded. "Lauren, is your mother in the house?" he asked me.

"No, sir — she started working this week," I answered.

"Maybe this kind of thing isn't such a good idea, with no adults at home," Officer Warner said, waving his hand at the garage and at the band.

"No, sir," I said. "Mrs. Sprouse is coming for them any minute now."

"Fine," said Officer Warner.

Please, please, please leave before my mom gets home, Officer Warner, I was thinking, fingers crossed. It wasn't five-thirty yet, so it should have been safe enough.

No such luck. Mom's car turned into the driveway at that very moment. She screeched to a stop when she saw the police car, and backed out into the street so that Officer Warner could get out.

They spoke for a few seconds on the sidewalk. Then Mom stormed across the yard.

"Lauren Hunter, just exactly what is going on here? I thought you said you were alone!"

"Alone in the *house*," I squeaked — my voice goes even higher than usual when I'm panicked. "The band needed a place to practice, and — "

"And who has been on the phone for the last thirty or forty minutes?" she interrupted me. "I was afraid something had happened to you when I couldn't get through!"

I'm not supposed to stay on the phone for more than ten minutes at a time.

"I haven't been talking to anyone," I said. "And no one's in the house except Kate. . . . Unless it's Brian?"

I had just remembered Brian. He wasn't in the garage.

"My little brother Brian?" Andy Hersh said.

I nodded. "Your mother dropped him off here to stay with you while she was at the doctor's," I said. "I thought he came out to the garage."

"If he's in your house, we'd better find him, quick," Andy said, hurrying toward the back steps. "He has this bad habit. . . ."

Mom and I followed Andy into the house, leaving Stephanie and the rest of the band standing around looking at each other.

Sure enough, we found Brian upstairs, sitting on the floor in the hall, the telephone receiver practically glued to his ear.

"Brian, is that what I think it is?" his big brother said sternly.

Brian grinned sheepishly. He handed the receiver to Andy, who listened for a second before hanging it up,

Andy shook his head. "Brian's memorized the number of one of those talk lines — you know, 480-GABB? — from hearing it on TV. And he calls whenever somebody isn't keeping an eye on him. I'm afraid he's probably run up your phone bill," Andy added. "It's a dollar for the first three minutes, and fifty cents for every minute after that. But if you let my mom know when the bill comes, she'll take care of it."

My mother didn't say anything then, but I could hear her foot tapping. The tapping foot meant I was really in for it later.

Kate appeared on the landing at that point. "Hi!" she said cheerfully. "Great movie! The yard's all empty. Did I miss anything?"

Chapter
9

Mom didn't say much until Dad got home from work that evening. Then she really let loose. "Obviously, Lauren is still too young to be on her own, even for a few hours after school," she said to my father.

That made me feel like a total baby — it was really embarrassing.

"It seems the only thing for me to do is get that baby-sitter we talked about," she went on.

"No, Mom — please *don't!*" I interrupted. "I'd *hate that!* I'll never let anyone in the house, or the yard, or the garage again. I won't even talk to anybody on the telephone between three-thirty and six. I'll do my chores, and my homework, and that's it."

Mom shook her head. "After today, I don't see

how I can trust you, Lauren. I was feeling sorry for you, picturing you all alone in the house, when in fact you had a yard full of strange kids, a rock band in the garage, and a police car in the driveway. Not to mention a four-year-old with expensive tastes using our phone."

"Ann, I think we have to at least give Lauren a chance to redeem herself," my dad said. "I'm sure she feels as badly about this as we do."

I *did*. And then I felt even worse, because the family conference ended with me being grounded for two whole weeks. Which meant that I would be taking the bus to and from Riverhurst Elementary every day — no biking with Kate, Patti, and Stephanie. No phoning, either, unless my parents were home. And *no sleepovers*.

"But this Friday the sleepover's supposed to be here," I said.

"Sorry," my dad said. "The girls will just have to work something else out for a couple of weeks."

As it turned out, I might not have had one that Friday anyway, because Stephanie wasn't speaking to me.

Since the school bus left my house at eight-ten, I got to school first the next morning. I was waiting near the bike rack when the others pedaled up. Stephanie climbed off her bike, jammed it into the rack, and walked away from me without saying a word.

"What's her problem?" I asked Kate and Patti.

"She thinks you ruined her chances to be another Lavonne," Patti said. "It sounds like you had an awful afternoon," she added sympathetically.

"I did. And my evening was even worse. But how can she be angry at me? Thanks to her, Officer Warner came to my house!" I said.

"You'd already unplugged Taylor," Kate said with a grin. "Wish I'd seen it!"

Stephanie marched straight up the sidewalk into the building. She was at her desk before the first bell rang. She never even looked up when Kate and I plopped down behind her.

At lunchtime, Stephanie carried her tray to the table where Tracy Osner was sitting with Sally Mason and some other fifth-graders.

"I don't care!" I said to Kate and Patti. "I'm twice as mad at her! *I'm* the one who's lost her allowance for weeks! *I'm* the one who's grounded!"

"It doesn't seem fair that Stephanie's blaming you when you're in all this trouble — and you were trying to help her to begin with," Patti said.

"I don't really get it, either," Kate agreed. "She must have been taking this whole singing idea a lot more seriously than we thought. And your parents are taking all this pretty seriously, too, aren't they? Are you really grounded, Lauren?"

"Totally. I can't even have the sleepover this Friday!"

"No sleepover?" Patti said. "'I can't have it at my house, either — Horace is having his whole Cub Scout troop over for camping in the attic."

"Since I had the last one, I probably can't have one again so soon . . . although my dad's on duty at the hospital all of Friday night and Saturday morning," Kate said.

I was feeling so crummy that I didn't much care *who* had it — I couldn't go, anyway. Taylor Sprouse was sitting on the other side of the cafeteria, but every so often, he'd lean forward to glare at me. Jenny Carlin and Angela Kemp strolled past our table just so Jenny could say, loud enough for me to hear, "And then when she slammed down the window. . . . It was *so* geeky!"

"Don't pay any attention to that airhead," Kate said, scowling at Jenny. "I bet you were great out there."

"And don't worry about Stephanie," Patti said

soothingly. "We'll talk to her. She'll get over it."

"Yeah, but will *I*?" I replied.

Thursday afternoon I rode the bus home. I did the chores Mom had written on her list: Vacuum the living room, wash a load of dark clothes, tear up a head of lettuce for salad. Then I did my homework. We had dinner. I watched some TV with my dad, and I went to bed.

Friday proceeded in pretty much the same way. I rode the bus to school. When I got there, Stephanie ignored me completely — it must be great to feel so sure of yourself. She sat with Tracy and Sally again in the cafeteria at lunch. I noticed her talking to Mark Freedman and Andy Hersh when Kate and Patti and I dropped off our trays.

"Maybe Fresh is giving her another try-out," Kate said.

When school was over that afternoon, I got back on the bus and rode home. I was so down that I hadn't even bothered to ask where the sleepover was that night. Maybe not knowing exactly where Kate and Patti and Stephanie were going to be would make it a tiny bit easier for me.

By about nine-thirty that evening, though, I'd started thinking about what they were doing. Had they gotten take-out from Mini's Italian Restaurant, or Mexican food from Pancho's Villa? Had Kate made super-fudge, or were they eating Mrs. Green's peanut-butter-chocolate-chip cookies?

Were they reading the advice column from *Teen Topics* out loud? Or were they checking out the newest Teen-Dream hunk in *Star Turns*?

I sighed and turned on my radio to listen to WBRM requests. On Friday and Saturday nights, you can call in to the Riverhurst radio station and dedicate a song to someone. It's mostly high-school kids who do it, but it's still fun to try to figure out who "T.K." is, or "L.J.M."

I wasn't really paying attention, though. I kept wondering why Kate and Patti hadn't called me at least, since I *could* talk on the phone when my parents were home. Three Sleepover Friends seemed to be enough for Stephanie. Were three enough for Kate and Patti, too?

At about ten-thirty, I went to bed, totally bummed out. I guess I was dreaming when I first heard the scratching noise, because it worked its way into my dream. A twenty-foot, twenty-pound alien from Venus, like the one we'd seen last month on Friday Chillers, was trying to tear the screen out of my window! I woke myself up just before I screamed, and looked at the clock. It was a little after midnight, around twelve-fifteen.

I turned over and closed my eyes again. *Scratch, scratch* . . . I sat up straight in bed . . . the noise was real! I pushed back the covers as quietly as I could. I slid out of bed and tiptoed slowly . . . slowly . . . to the window on the far wall of my room.

I *do* let my thoughts run away with me from time to time, and I was imagining all kinds of creepy things. But not the thing I saw when I pulled back the curtain — it was too wild even for me! A shiny, silvery, four-fingered . . . CLAW! I was too scared to do anything but squeak. I wanted to get my dad, but my feet seemed to be stuck to the floor.

That's when a voice floated up from below: ''Lau-ren!''

I peered through the window again. The claw was gone, so I looked straight down. Kate, Stephanie, and Patti were standing in my side yard, holding a long silver pole!

They waved for me to come down.

What did I have to lose? Certainly not my allowance! I pulled some sweatpants and a sweater on over my pajamas and crept downstairs.

Roger's room is on the first floor, past the den. Bullwinkle sleeps in there, too. Luckily, Bullwinkle didn't hear me. Maybe Fresh had made him temporarily deaf. I sneaked down the hall to the kitchen, carefully unlocked the back door, and opened it without a click. I closed it softly behind me and looked around. "Kate?" I whispered.

The three of them dashed around the side of the house. Along with the pole, they were carrying two big shopping bags.

"What are you doing here?" I said.

"What does it look like?" Stephanie answered. "Having our sleepover."

"We sneaked out," said Patti.

"Let's go into the garage," Kate suggested. "I'm cold out here."

We squeezed between the sliding doors, and then around my parents' cars. Kate had brought a flashlight, so we could see well enough to pull some bags of peat moss into a circle to sit on. Then Kate and Patti started unpacking the shopping bags.

"Lauren's special dip," Kate announced, setting the bowl down on a napkin. "Chili-flavored potato chips, Mrs. Green's peanut-butter-chocolate-chip cookies. . . ."

"Hold it!" I was starving. I'd been sort of off my feed for the last couple of days, but now my appetite was coming back like gangbusters. There was something I had to know first, though. "What was that silver claw?" I asked. "Or were you just trying to scare me to death?"

"Claw?" Kate looked puzzled. Then she giggled. "Oh — my dad uses it to scoop leaves out of the gutter below our roof. It was the only thing long enough to reach your window."

"Dr Pepper," Patti was saying as she unloaded her shopping bag. "A thermos of ice. Paper cups. Fudge-ripple ice cream. Paper bowls. Spoons."

It was a real feast. We did a lot more eating than talking. I had lots of everything, so much that Kate said, "That stomach of yours in outer space? It's going to get so heavy that it'll knock its planet out of orbit. And then where will you be?"

"Lauren," Stephanie said suddenly, "I'm really sorry about the way I've been acting."

"Oh, that's okay," I said.

"No, it isn't," Stephanie said. "Patti and Kate talked to me this afternoon, but I think I'd already realized I was being a jerk. I took advantage of the fact that you're nice and easy-going, and kind of forced you into letting Fresh practice here.''

"The tie-dyeing, too," Kate reminded her.

I didn't say anything, but I thought Stephanie was right.

"Then I blamed you for ruining my singing career, when really I didn't *have* a singing career," Stephanie went on.

"I was probably wrong about — " I started out, but Stephanie kept going.

"I talked to Mark and Andy today. Taylor Sprouse has already told Wendy Rodwin she can sing with the band if she lets them practice at her house.''

"Oh," I said.

"You were right, Lauren — he didn't really want me. He doesn't want a girl singer. He just wants a place to practice," Stephanie finished. "Anyway, I felt awful when you and I weren't speaking. And I just wanted to tell you that you were right, and I was wrong, and I'm sorry all my careers have gotten you in so much trouble. Friends?''

"You bet — Sleepover Friends forever!" I said.

"Yay!" Kate and Patti cheered softly.

I got up to give Stephanie a hug . . . and that's when I tripped over the rake. It crashed into the shovels my dad had leaned against the wall, which fell, clanging against the wheelbarrow.

Not even damaged eardrums could keep Bullwinkle from hearing that. He started barking like crazy inside the house.

"Uh-oh," Patti said.

"I think the party's over," said Stephanie. She reached into one of the shopping bags and pulled out a tie-dyed T-shirt. "For you, Lauren — I made one for each of us."

"Let's get out of here," Kate said, hurrying us toward the garage doors.

She waited until Patti and Stephanie had squeezed into the hedge between my house and Donald Foster's. Then she whispered to me, "One good thing came out of this."

"What?" I asked her.

"You know you can get tough when you need to! See you!" Kate pushed into the bushes behind Patti and Stephanie, and I raced back to my house.

I'd just gotten the back door locked when my father called sleepily from upstairs, "What's going on down there?"

"It's just me, Dad," I called back, giving Bullwinkle's thick neck a squeeze. "I woke up hungry."

"Well, please quiet that dog down."

"I will!" I opened the refrigerator, pulled out some leftover tuna noodle casserole, and gave Bullwinkle a big spoonful.

Then I took off my sweater and pulled on the tie-dyed T-shirt. It had a scarlet background and every color of the rainbow in the center. It was gorgeous!

Sleepover Friends forever!

#15 Stephanie's Big Story

As soon as Stephanie and I stepped out the front door of the school, we saw Jenny Carlin and Angela Kemp sitting on one of the benches near the playground.

"She doesn't look nearly as perky as she did this morning, does she?" Stephanie said thoughtfully.

In fact, Jenny's mean little face was screwed up into a major scowl.

Then Stephanie actually called out, "Hey, Jenny — did you get it, or not? Are you Ms. X, the new advice columnist for our school paper?" I couldn't believe it!

"Buzz off, Stephanie!" Jenny screeched. "You, too, Lauren Hunter!"

Win the sleeping bag of your dreams!

Enter the
SLEEPOVER FRIENDS
SLEEPING BAG GIVEAWAY!

50 WINNERS!

Your sleepover party won't be complete without a Sleepover Friends sleeping bag! Now you can enter the Sleepover Friends Giveaway and win a roomy (28″ x 57″), comfy sleeping bag! All you have to do is complete the coupon below and return by October 31, 1989.

This soft, plush sleeping bag is pink and has an adorable white sheep pattern on the inside. It is washable, has a heavy-duty zipper, and elastic straps that make it easy to roll up and compact to carry. Bring it to your next sleepover party and have the best time ever! Kate, Lauren, Stephanie, and Patti always have a great party in their series packed with fun and adventure–the **Sleepover Friends!**

Rules: Entries must be postmarked by October 31, 1989. Contestants must be between the ages of 7 and 12. Winners will be picked at random from all eligible entries received. No purchase necessary. Valid only in the U.S.A. Employees of Scholastic Inc., affiliates, subsidiaries, and their families are not eligible. Void where prohibited. Winners will be notified by mail.

Fill in your name, age, and address below or write the information on a 3″ x 5″ piece of paper and mail to: SLEEPOVER FRIENDS GIVEAWAY, Scholastic Inc., P.O. Box 673, Cooper Station, New York, NY 10276.

Sleepover Friends Sleeping Bag Giveaway
Where did you buy this Sleepover Friends book?

☐ Bookstore   ☐ Drug Store   ☐ Supermarket
☐ Discount Store   ☐ Book Club   ☐ Book Fair
☐ Other _____ _____
            specify

Name _____

Birthday_____Age _____

Street _____

City, State, Zip _____

SLE1288